ANIMAL LOOK-ALIKES

SEAL OR SEA LION?

By Rob Ryndak

Gareth Stevens
PUBLISHING

Please visit our website, www.garethstevens.com. For a free color catalog of all our high-quality books, call toll free 1-800-542-2595 or fax 1-877-542-2596.

Library of Congress Cataloging-in-Publication Data

Ryndak, Rob, author.
 Seal or sea lion? / Rob Ryndak.
    pages cm. — (Animal look-alikes)
 Includes bibliographical references and index.
 ISBN 978-1-4824-2724-0 (pbk.)
 ISBN 978-1-4824-2725-7 (6 pack)
 ISBN 978-1-4824-2726-4 (library binding)
 1. Seals (Animals)—Juvenile literature. 2. Sea lions—Juvenile literature. [1. Pinnipeds.] I. Title.
 QL737.P64R96 2016
 599.79—dc23

                                        2015008465

Published in 2016 by
Gareth Stevens Publishing
111 East 14th Street, Suite 349
New York, NY 10003

Designer: Sarah Liddell
Editor: Ryan Nagelhout

Photo credits: Cover, p. 1 (background) MIMOHE/Shutterstock.com; cover, p. 1 (seal and sea lion) Eric Isselee/Shutterstock.com; p. 5 Andrea Izzotti/Shutterstock.com; p. 7 (sea lion) chbaum/Shutterstock.com; p. 7 (seal) Ulrike Jordan/Shutterstock.com; p. 7 (walrus) Vladimir Melnik/Shutterstock.com; p. 9 (top) Simone Janssen/Shutterstock.com; p. 9 (bottom) Christian Musat/Shutterstock.com; p. 11 (top) Joshua Sharp/Shutterstock.com; p. 11 Barnes Ian/Shutterstock.com; p. 13 (bottom) Khoroshunova Olga/Shutterstock.com; p. 13 (top) wim claes/Shutterstock.com; p. 15 (seal) Jose Gil/Shutterstock.com; p. 15 (sea lion) MindStorm/Shutterstock.com; p. 17 (main) Blaine Image/Shutterstock.com; p. 17 (map) Ivsanmas/Shutterstock.com; p. 19 Dmytro Pylypenko/Shutterstock.com; p. 21 Sylvain Cordier/Stone/Getty Images.

Printed in the United States of America

CPSIA compliance information: Batch #CS15GS: For further information contact Gareth Stevens, New York, New York at 1-800-542-2595.

CONTENTS

Boldface words appear in the glossary.

Sea... Something

Seals and sea lions look very much alike. Many live in the same places, and they both love the water. They are often called "second cousins," but the two are very different. Let's find out how to tell them apart!

5

Seals, sea lions, and walruses all come from an animal group called pinnipeds. Pinnipeds are **mammals** that live both in water and on land, eat sea creatures, and breathe air. Sea lions are in the Otariidae family, while seals are part of the Phocidae family.

SEA LION

SEAL

WALRUS

7

Head Games

The easiest way to tell a seal and sea lion apart is by looking at their ears. Sea lions have small earflaps on the sides of their heads. Seals have tiny openings for their ears, but nothing that sticks out.

Flipper Fun

Seals have short, hairy **foreflippers** with claws on them. Sea lions have longer foreflippers that don't have hair or claws. Both mammals have a thick **layer** of **blubber** to keep them warm. They also both love to eat fish!

SEAL

SEA LION

Seals and sea lions move differently, too. Sea lions can turn their **hindflippers** under their body so they can walk on land. Seals **wriggle** or slide along on their belly to move on land. In the water, they swim with their hindflippers, using their foreflippers to steer. Sea lions push through the water using their foreflippers.

SEAL

SEA LION

Together or Alone?

Seals live alone and spend more time in water than sea lions. They only **mate** with other seals once a year on land. Sea lions are much more social and spend more time on land. They can live together in groups of more than 1,500!

SEAL

SEA LION

HOW CAN YOU TELL?

ANIMAL	SEAL	SEA LION
FAMILY	Phocidae	Otariidae
LAND OR SEA?	better in water	better on land
EARS	earholes	earflaps
FLIPPERS	short, hairy with claws	long, hairless
NOISES	soft grunts	loud barks
MOVEMENT ON LAND	wriggle or slide on belly	move hindflippers under body to walk
HOW THEY SWIM	hindflippers, steering with foreflippers	foreflippers

15

Where They Live

Seals and sea lions both live on the western coasts of the United States and Canada. Seals also live near the North and South Poles, Greenland, and the **continent** of Antarctica. Sea lions live on the southern coasts of South America, Africa, and Australia and in the Pacific Ocean.

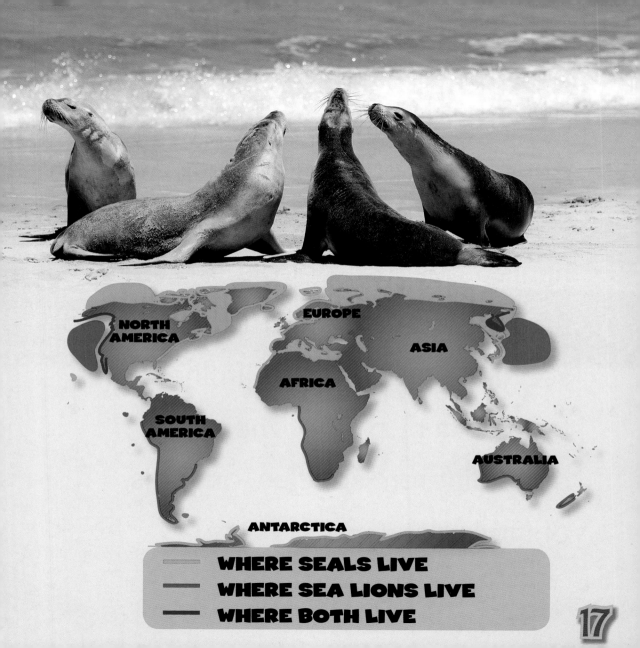

NORTH
AMERICA

EUROPE

ASIA

AFRICA

SOUTH
AMERICA

AUSTRALIA

ANTARCTICA

WHERE SEALS LIVE

WHERE SEA LIONS LIVE

WHERE BOTH LIVE

17

What Are Fur Seals?

Animals called fur seals are actually sea lions! These animals are often hunted because people like their fur. Fur seals have earflaps like sea lions and also live in the water for weeks at a time. There are eight different species, or kinds, of fur seals.

FUR SEAL

19

Seals and sea lions may be different, but they're both food for some animals. Sharks, orcas, and polar bears all eat them. That means seals and sea lions have to watch where they swim, or they might be dinner!

GLOSSARY

blubber: a layer of fat on a sea mammal's body

continent: one of Earth's seven great landmasses

foreflipper: a limb on the front of a seal or sea lion

hindflipper: the back flipper of a seal or sea lion

layer: one thickness of something lying over or under another

mammal: a warm-blooded animal that has a backbone and hair, breathes air, and feeds milk to its young

mate: to come together to make babies

wriggle: to twist or move back and forth like a worm

FOR MORE INFORMATION

BOOKS

Rockwood, Leigh. *Tell Me the Difference Between a Seal and a Sea Lion.* New York, NY: PowerKids Press, 2013.

Silverman, Buffy. *Can You Tell a Seal from a Sea Lion?* Minneapolis, MN: Lerner, 2012.

WEBSITES

Sea Lion vs. Seal
dolphinencounters.com/education-sealionvsseal.php
Get more facts about seals and sea lions, and see how they are different here.

What's the Difference Between Seals and Sea Lions?
nmlc.org/2011/06/whats-the-difference-between-seals-and-sea-lions/
Find out more about seals and sea lions on this National Marine Life Center website.

INDEX